To your family from ours,

I loved illustrating this Book, it gave me a chance to bring Bill's sweet story of hope to life.

Bruce, Tina Marie and Annie Bowlsbey
(Santa Catalina School)

The Adventures of LC, the Lucky Calf

Written by Bill Pereira
Illustrated by Tina Marie Bowlsby

Published by Little Tule Books
P.O. Box 549
Carmel Valley, CA 93924
www.LittleTuleBooks.com

Published in 2005 by Little Tule Books.

ISBN 0-9773133-0-1

Copyright Bill Pereira, 2005.

All rights reserved.

Printed in the United States of America.

Art and Technical Production, Lynne Frey.

"Hope is the thing with wings that perches in the soul."
Emily Dickinson

Carmel Valley is filled with fragrant forests, clear streams, and hidden canyons. Bands of lupines streak the meadows in spring, and acres of native grasses grow in summer. Birdsongs fill the air during the day. Coyotes yip at night. Surrounded by steep foothills that rise into the Santa Lucia Mountains, Carmel Valley remains pristine ranching country.

Carmel Valley was home to Native Americans for centuries before the first land grants were settled in the 1800s. The Little Tule Ranch has remained much the same for two hundred years. The first rancher built his adobe house on a knoll where a great oak tree grew. Bill Pereira is now steward of what has been called the most beautiful land in the Valley. The knoll has become a focal point of life on Little Tule Ranch, a grassy bed where cows go to give birth under the great oak tree.

In *Little Tule Books*, Rancher Bill tells true stories of the animals he cares for.

Little Tule Ranch sits high in the mountains, overlooking the Pacific Ocean. Cows and their calves graze the gentle hills and rest in the meadows.

They are taken care of by Bill, the rancher.

LC, a Hereford heifer calf, was born
under the giant oak tree on the green pastures
of Little Tule Ranch. LC stands for 'Lucky Calf,'
the name given to the calf by Rancher Bill.
And as it turns out, LC was very lucky indeed!

3

LC was born on a cold and foggy night in early spring.

LC sat quietly in the deep grass waiting for her mother to return. She was all alone, curled up tightly under the giant oak tree.

The coyotes yelped loudly at sunrise and sunset. **LC** was lonely and scared.

5

A great red-tailed hawk screeched as it circled overhead.

Without her mother's milk, **LC** grew weaker and weaker.

She heard an unfamiliar whistling and a faint tinkling noise. Something was coming toward her. A giant shadow settled over her, and two big arms lifted her from the deep grass. **LC's** eyes grew wide with fear, and she cried out for her mother.

LC's luck had started to change. The big arms holding her were gentle. A very friendly black animal covered her with wet kisses. **LC** had just met Bill, the rancher, and Drake, Bill's Labrador Retriever.

Bill had a bottle of warm milk for **LC**, and she suckled that bottle like there was no tomorrow. Drake stayed close by, licking the milk that dripped from her mouth.

Rancher Bill and Drake got up very early every day to feed and care for **LC**. As the calf grew, she gained weight and strength.

Soon **LC** was playing with Drake, bucking and jumping. She looked forward to Rancher Bill and Drake coming to her pen.

LC could hear other cows and calves in the pasture. She wanted to join them.

One day, LC pushed open the gate of her pen. She looked around the barnyard for Rancher Bill and Drake. They were nowhere in sight. LC crossed the barnyard and went to the fence of the big pasture.

15

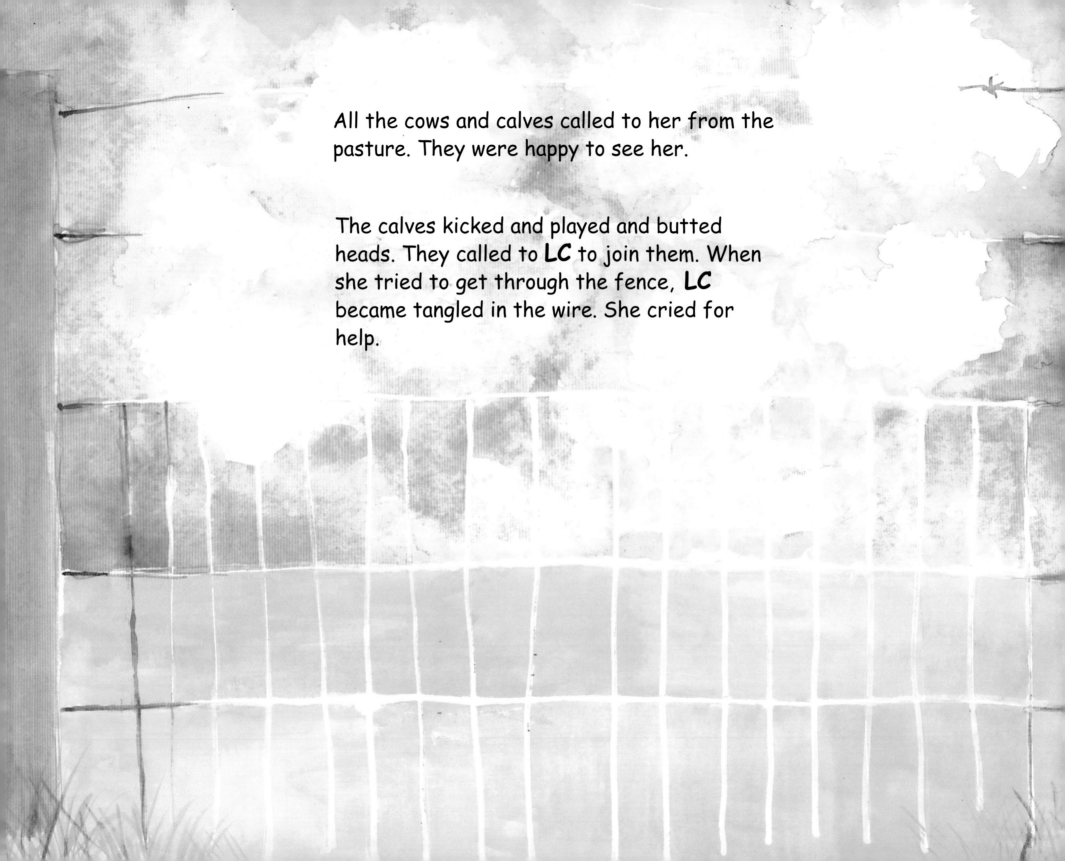

All the cows and calves called to her from the pasture. They were happy to see her.

The calves kicked and played and butted heads. They called to **LC** to join them. When she tried to get through the fence, **LC** became tangled in the wire. She cried for help.

LC heard the familiar whistling and tinkling. Soon Rancher Bill arrived and helped to untangle her head from the fence.

LC licked Rancher Bill's hand with thanks and kissed Drake. The three of them walked back to the barn, where **LC** drank warm milk.

One day, Rancher Bill led **LC** through the gate and out into the big pasture. **LC** could not remember a more joyous day. All the other calves were happy to see **LC**. They ran and played together.

The butterflies flitted above the calves, and barn swallows swooped through the sky.

Life in the big pasture was as wonderful as **LC** had imagined!

21

As evening came, the calves went to
their mothers and began to nurse.

LC watched with sadness. She wanted to nurse too, but the cows did not share their milk with **LC**.

23

Soon the pasture grew dark and fog rolled in, covering **LC** in a cold, misty blanket. All the other calves nestled with their mothers to stay warm. **LC** had no one.

LC heard the coyotes and owls as night fell. **LC** became colder and more frightened.

25

Then **LC** heard the familiar whistling and tinkling. Rancher Bill appeared out of the darkness. He gently picked up **LC** in his strong, warm arms and carried her to the barn. Rancher Bill used his coat to dry the rain from **LC** and laid the coat across her.

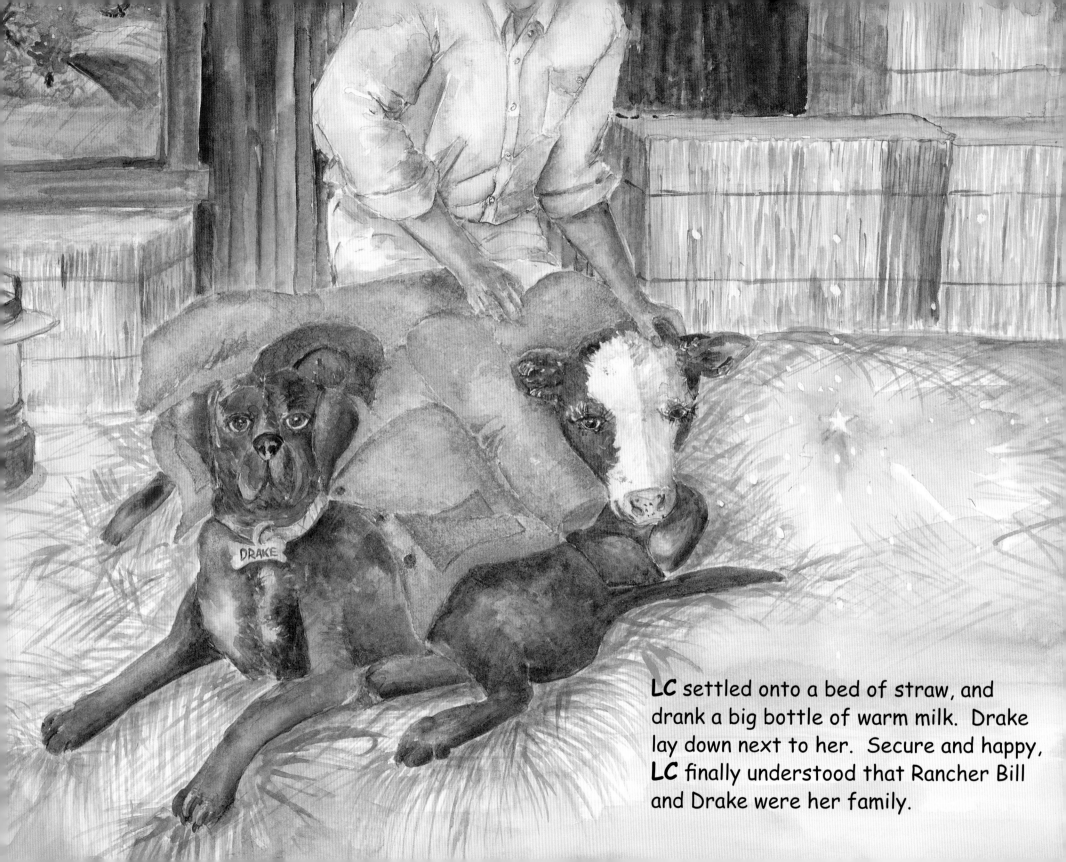

LC settled onto a bed of straw, and drank a big bottle of warm milk. Drake lay down next to her. Secure and happy, **LC** finally understood that Rancher Bill and Drake were her family.

Questions for Rancher Bill

In the story there is reference to "whistling and tinkling." Can you explain?
Yes! I whistle while I work. The cows that I take care of have become accustomed to the whistling and are reassured by the sound. The "tinkling" sound comes from my constant companion Drake, who wears a big red collar with noisy tags that tinkle.

What is a tule?
A tule is also known as a cattail or bulrush. The plants grow in places with a constant supply of water. The ranch was named after the tules that grow along the banks of the lake. The ranch has always been a source for water that feeds the Carmel River. Water is a very important resource for ranchers.

Did LC ever find her Mother?
Yes, **LC** finds her Mother! **LC** begins a search for her Mother with Drake and all of the wild animals on the ranch pitching in!

LC was a twin. Twins are rare but not unheard of. Often times a mother cow will become confused and allow only one of the twins to nurse. The remaining calf is abandoned. The first several hours of a calf's life are critical for its survival. Rancher Bill is always on the lookout for abandoned calves during calving season.

Calves need constant care, with feedings every 3 hours. It takes a great effort for a rancher to care for an abandoned calf, considering his demanding schedule. Abandoned calves become the ranch's pet and are a lot like dogs, coming to whistles and demanding attention that the other cows don't demand.

Does Drake really exist?
Yes, Drake is my constant companion and even though he is a Labrador Retriever (which is a water dog), he thinks he is a cow dog.

Where is LC now?
LC is out in the pasture with her friends. I can see her from my front window even though the pasture is very large.